STORIES FOR
THE VERY YOUNG

STORIES FOR
THE VERY YOUNG

Collected by Susan Dickinson

Illustrated by Kate Aldous

LIBER PRESS

*First published 1992 by
Liber Press, Cuttlebrook House,
Charlton Village, OX12 7HE, England*

An Albion Book

*Conceived, designed and produced by
The Albion Press Ltd, P.O. Box 52,
Princes Risborough, Aylesbury, Bucks*

*Designer: Emma Bradford
Project Manager: Elizabeth Wilkes
Permissions: Nick Wetton*

*Selection copyright © 1992 Susan Dickinson
Illustrations copyright © 1992 Kate Aldous
Volume copyright © 1992 The Albion Press Ltd*

ISBN 1 85734 012 4

*Typesetting and colour origination by York House, London
Printed and bound in Italy by New Interlitho*

ACKNOWLEDGEMENTS

*Thanks are due to the copyright holders of the following stories for
permission to reprint them in this volume:*

Floella Benjamin: to Random Century Group for "Why the Agouti Has No Tail" from *Why the Agouti Has
No Tail and Other Stories* (Hutchinson Ltd); Lilian Daykin: to Eileen Colwell on behalf of the author for
"The Little Woman's Water-Pot" from *The Youngest Story Book*, edited by Eileen Colwell (The Bodley
Head); Dorothy Edwards: to Octopus Publishing Group Library and Houghton Mifflin Co. for "My
Naughty Little Sister and Father Christmas" ("The Naughtiest Story of All") from *My Naughty Little Sister*
(Methuen Children's Books); Terry Jones: to Pavilion Books for "The Butterfly Who Sang" from *Fairy
Tales*; Joan G. Robinson: to Harrap Publishing Group Ltd for "Mary-Mary and the Snow Giant" from
More Mary-Mary (Harrap Publishing Group Ltd); Carl Sandburg: to Harcourt Brace Jovanovich Inc. for
"How the Hat Ashes Shovel Helped Snoo Foo" from *Rootabaga Stories*, copyright 1922 by Harcourt Brace
Jovanovich, Inc. and renewed 1950 by Carl Sandburg; David Thomson: to Penguin Books Ltd for
"Danny Fox Steals Some Fish" from *Danny Fox* (Puffin Books, 1966),
copyright © David Thomson, 1966

*While every effort has been made to find copyright holders, this has not always been possible, and
The Albion Press, in care of the publishers, will be glad to make good any omissions in future editions.*

CONTENTS

THE LION AND THE MOUSE

Aesop

RETOLD BY SUSAN DICKINSON

A Lion was once lying asleep under a tree. Unfortunately his great body was blocking the entrance to the hole of a little Mouse and the Mouse was running up and down trying to find a way in, when the Lion woke up.

"Aaargh!" he roared. "What are you doing, waking me up like this?" And he placed his huge paw over the Mouse and opened his jaws to swallow him up.

"Oh! I beg your pardon," cried the Mouse. "Please forgive me and let me go. Who knows, maybe one day I shall be able to do you a good turn."

The Lion laughed. "You?" he said. "How could you, a mere mouse, help me, the King of the Beasts?" But he lifted his paw and let the Mouse go.

Time passed, and one day the Mouse heard a terrible roaring and snarling in the forest. On going to investigate, he found the Lion caught fast in a huge net.

"Help me, help me," said the Lion. "The hunters who have trapped me have gone to fetch a wagon to carry me away alive to the King. Who knows what will become of me?"

The Mouse ran up the Lion's shoulder and whispered in his ear, "Stay still and I will set you free."

Then the Mouse gnawed away at the ropes that bound the Lion until one by one they fell away and the Lion was free.

"Thank you, thank you, little friend," said the Lion. "You were quite right. You have done me a good turn. I never imagined that such a small creature would be able to help me, the King of the Beasts."

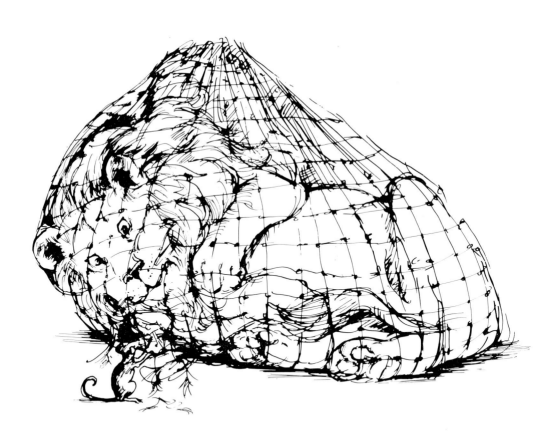

JOHNNY-CAKE

An English folktale

RETOLD BY JOSEPH JACOBS

Once upon a time there was an old man, and an old woman, and a little boy. One morning the old woman made a Johnny-cake, and put it in the oven to bake. "You watch the Johnny-cake while your father and I go out to work in the garden." So the old man and the old woman went out and began to hoe potatoes, and left the little boy to tend the oven. But he didn't watch it all the time, and all of a sudden he heard a noise, and he looked up and the oven door popped open, and out of the oven jumped Johnny-cake, and went rolling along end over end towards the open door of the house. The little boy ran to shut the door, but Johnny-cake was too quick for him and rolled through the door, down the steps, and out into the road long before the little boy could catch him. The little boy ran after him as fast as he could, crying out to his father and mother, who heard the uproar and threw down their hoes and gave chase too. But Johnny-cake outran all three a long way, and was soon out of sight, while they had to sit down, all out of breath, on a bank to rest.

On went Johnny-cake, and by-and-by he came to two well-diggers who looked up from their work and called out: "Where are ye going, Johnny-cake?"

He said: "I've outrun an old man, and an old woman, and a little boy, and I can outrun you too-o-o!"

"Ye can, can ye? We'll see about that!" said they, and they threw down their picks and ran after him, but couldn't catch up with him, and soon they had to sit down by the roadside to rest.

On ran Johnny-cake, and by-and-by he came to two ditch-diggers who were digging a ditch. "Where are ye going, Johnny-cake?" said they. He said: "I've outrun an old man, and an old woman, and a little boy, and two well-diggers, and I can outrun you too-o-o!"

"Ye can, can ye? We'll see about that!" said they, and they threw down their spades and ran after him too. But Johnny-cake soon outstripped them also, and seeing they could never catch him, they gave up the chase and sat down to rest.

On went Johnny-cake, and by-and-by he came to a bear. The bear said: "Where are ye going, Johnny-cake?"

He said: "I've outrun an old man, and an old woman, and a little boy, and two well-diggers, and two ditch-diggers, and I can outrun you too-o-o!"

"Ye can, can ye?" growled the bear, "we'll see about that!" And he trotted as fast as his legs could carry him

after Johnny-cake, who never stopped to look behind him. Before long the bear was left so far behind that he saw he might as well give up the hunt first as last, so he stretched himself out by the roadside to rest.

On went Johnny-cake, and by-and-by he came to a wolf. The wolf said: "Where are ye going, Johnny-cake?"

He said: "I've outrun an old man, and an old woman, and a little boy, and two well-diggers, and two ditch-diggers, and a bear, and I can outrun you too-o-o!"

"Ye can, can ye?" snarled the wolf. "We'll see about that!" And he set into a gallop after Johnny-cake, who went on and on so fast that the wolf too saw there was no hope of overtaking him, and he too lay down to rest.

On went Johnny-cake, and by-and-by he came to a fox that lay quietly in a corner of the fence. The fox called out in a sharp voice, but without getting up: "Where are ye going, Johnny-cake?"

He said: "I've outrun an old man, and an old woman, and a little boy, and two well-diggers, and two ditch-diggers, and a bear, and a wolf, and I can outrun you too-o-o!"

The fox said: "I can't quite hear you, Johnny-cake, won't you come a little closer?" turning his head a little to one side.

Johnny-cake stopped his race for the first time, and went a little closer, and called out in a very loud voice: *"I've outrun an old man, and an old woman, and a little boy, and two well-diggers, and two ditch-diggers, and a bear, and a wolf, and I can outrun you too-o-o!''*

''Can't quite hear you; won't you come a *little* closer?'' said the fox in a feeble voice, as he stretched out his neck towards Johnny-cake, and put one paw behind his ear.

Johnny-cake came up close, and leaning towards the fox screamed out: ''I'VE OUTRUN AN OLD MAN, AND AN OLD WOMAN, AND A LITTLE BOY, AND TWO WELL-DIGGERS, AND TWO DITCH-DIGGERS, AND A BEAR, AND A WOLF, AND I CAN OUTRUN YOU TOO-O-O!''

''You can, can you?'' yelped the fox, and he snapped up the Johnny-cake in his sharp teeth in the twinkling of an eye.

MONDAY'S CHILD IS FAIR OF FACE

Traditional

Monday's child is fair of face,
Tuesday's child is full of grace,
Wednesday's child is full of woe,
Thursday's child has far to go,
Friday's child is loving and giving,
Saturday's child works hard for its living,
But the child that is born on the Sabbath day
Is bonny and blithe, and good and gay.

18

WHY THE AGOUTI HAS NO TAIL

Floella Benjamin

An agouti is a small animal that lives in the West Indies. It looks something like a squirrel, only it doesn't have a tail. A long time ago, however, the agouti did have a fine tail and this is the story of how it lost it.

Once upon a time the dog and the agouti were very good friends and lived together happily. One day Agouti and Dog were lazing in the garden, enjoying the afternoon sun when along came Goat, who was looking very pleased with himself.

"What are you so happy about?" asked Dog.

"I've been invited to a party," replied Goat with satisfaction.

Now, both Dog and Agouti loved parties and when they heard this their ears pricked up.

"What party is this?" said Agouti. "We want to come as well,"

"Oh, *you* can't come," said Goat haughtily. "This party is only for animals which have horns." Then he trotted off with his head in the air.

Dog and Agouti looked at each other. Neither of them had horns and that meant that they would definitely

19

not be going to the party.

"Oh, dear," said Dog. "I do love parties; there is always lots of food to eat."

"This has spoilt my whole day," said Agouti, and he went indoors to sulk.

The next day Dog and Agouti went into town. The news of the party had spread and everyone was talking about it, especially the animals with horns. Apparently, the party was to be held on a small island some distance away. There was to be a barbecue and lots of rum-punch to drink. All the horned animals were to leave for the island, by boat, the next morning and return in the evening after the party.

"It's not fair," said Dog. "I must find a way to go to the party."

"But you don't have horns," said Agouti. "You would soon be spotted and then there would be trouble."

"Don't worry, I will find a way," said Dog, and he disappeared into the forest, leaving his friend Agouti behind.

Dog walked along a narrow path which led through the trees. He just had to think of a way to get invited to the party, but however hard he thought, he couldn't come up with any ideas.

Suddenly, as he rounded a corner, he saw a pile of old bones in front of him on the path. They were the remains of a cow that had died many years ago.

What luck, thought Dog, as he spotted a lovely pair of horns amongst the pile of bones. He picked them up

and tied them to his head with a strong piece of vine. Then he rushed home to show his friend Agouti.

But Agouti was not very pleased when he saw Dog with the horns. "It's all right for you. You are large enough to pass as a horned animal. But what about me? I would soon be spotted. There are no horned animals as small as I am. I still can't go to the party." Agouti was more miserable than ever and he sat in a corner and sulked.

The next morning Dog was up bright and early. He tied the horns to his head as tightly as he could. "Come down to the jetty with me, Agouti," he pleaded, "and see if my disguise works."

Reluctantly, Agouti agreed. He was interested to see if Dog could get away with the deception.

The jetty was bustling with horned animals, all waiting for the boat to arrive and take them across to the island. So none of them noticed as Dog, wearing his horns, slipped quietly amongst them.

Agouti watched as Dog climbed aboard the boat and sat down next to Goat. His heart beat faster, as he realized that his best friend was going to get away with the trick and go to the party without him. He was so jealous that, before he could stop himself, he cried out, "Stop! Stop! There is an imposter aboard."

At this, all the horned animals looked at Dog and saw that he had tricked them. They picked him up angrily and threw him into the water.

When Agouti realized what his jealous betrayal had done, he turned and ran as fast as he could, with Dog close on his heels. He ran and ran as fast as his short legs could carry him, but Dog was angry and humiliated and soon caught up with Agouti, who scurried into a nearby hole. But Agouti wasn't quite fast enough and Dog snapped off his tail as he disappeared down the hole.

Well, needless to say, Dog and Agouti were no longer friends, and if you are ever in the West Indies and you see a dog scratching and barking at a hole, it is probably because there is an agouti down there. That is how the agouti lost its tail.

THE HARE AND THE TORTOISE

Aesop

RETOLD BY SUSAN DICKINSON

There was once a Hare who loved to boast that he could run faster than any of the other animals. "I can beat any of you!" he proclaimed, with a swagger. "I challenge anyone here to race against me."

The other animals looked at each other. Who would accept the Hare's challenge?

Then the Tortoise spoke up. "I will race against you," he said.

"You!" cried the Hare. "Don't be ridiculous! I shall be at the winning post before you've even started."

"Do you agree to race, or not?" asked the Tortoise quietly.

"OK. OK." said the Hare. "Where shall we race?"

Everybody started to argue as to where the race should be held. But at last it was agreed. The Hare and the Tortoise would run from the farm gate, across the meadow to the stile, around the carrot field to the gap in the hedge and finish at the scarecrow in the middle of the wheatfield.

The next day everybody lined up to watch the start. "Ready! Steady! Go!" cried the cock.

The Hare streamed away across the meadow towards the stile, and the Tortoise started over the short grass. When the Hare reached the carrot field he said to himself, "Just as I knew it, the Tortoise has hardly started, and I am already nearly at the finish. I have plenty of time for lunch before he even crosses the meadow."

So saying, the Hare pulled up several juicy carrots and scrunched away merrily. Carrots were one of his favourite vegetables. Then he pulled up some more, and soon he was feeling so full and fat that he ambled over to the hedge where he fell asleep in the shade.

Meanwhile, the Tortoise was still plodding across the meadow, and when he reached the stile the sun was high in the sky. He began to make his way around the edge of the carrot field. He plodded on and plodded on and in a while what should he see but the Hare, fast asleep. On went the Tortoise until he reached the gap

in the hedge. Now he could see the scarecrow waving his arms in the middle of the wheatfield.

The sun began to drop lower in the sky and the Hare woke up with a snort. He jumped to his feet and bounded along the hedge to the gap.

Now he too could see the scarecrow standing waiting for him. But what was this? A crowd was gathered, cheering and shouting: ''Hurry up! You're winning! Come on! Come on!''

The Hare galloped across the wheatfield as fast as he could. But too late! The Tortoise reached the scarecrow just in front of him.

And so the slow and steady Tortoise won the race against the foolish, boastful Hare.

I LOVE LITTLE PUSSY

Traditional

I love little pussy, her coat is so warm,
And if I don't hurt her she'll do me no harm.
So I'll not pull her tail nor drive her away,
But pussy and I very gently will play.
She'll sit by my side, and I'll give her some food,
And she'll love me because I am gentle and good.

MARY-MARY AND THE SNOW GIANT

Joan G. Robinson

One day Mary-Mary woke up and found that some more snow had fallen in the night. There had been snow for two or three days, but it had all got trampled and dirty. Now there was a new white covering over everything. It looked very pretty.

Mary-Mary decided to go out before breakfast and be the very first person to make foot prints in the new snow. She dressed quickly and quietly, put on her coat and crept downstairs. In the hall she found Father's boots.

"Just the thing," said Mary-Mary to herself. "I shall feel like a proper snow giant in those." And she stepped inside them, shoes and all, and went quietly out into the back garden. And nobody else knew anything about it at all.

At breakfast-time Mary-Mary's big brothers and sisters were all very excited, talking about the new snow.

"Let's divide the lawn into four," said Miriam; "then we can each have our own part. I shall make a snow palace in mine."

"Good idea," said Martyn. "I shall make a big white horse in mine."

"I shall make an igloo and be an Eskimo," said Mervyn.

"And I shall make a snow queen," said Meg.

Mary-Mary said, "I shall do something better than all of those. I shall make a snow giant."

But Miriam said, "No, we can't divide the lawn into five."

And Martyn said, "You messed it all up last time, making snowballs and things."

And Mervyn said, "You go round the edges or play in the front."

And Meg said, "Anyway, there isn't any such thing as a snow giant."

"Oh, yes, there is!" said Mary-Mary.

"Oh, no, there isn't," said all the others.

Mary-Mary looked at them all and said slowly, in her most important grown-up voice, "There's been a snow giant in the garden already this morning."

"Rubbish," they said. "We don't believe it."

"Moppet knows there was a snow giant," said Mary-Mary. "Don't you, Moppet?" Then she squeaked, "Yes," in Moppet's voice.

But the others just said, "Nonsense. Don't take any notice of her." Then they all went off to put on their coats and Wellingtons, and go out in the garden.

Mary-Mary stayed in the kitchen with Mother and helped to put away the spoons and forks. In a minute Martyn came to the back door and said, "Mother, has anyone been in our garden?"

"No," said Mother, "not this morning."

"Not Father even?" said Martyn.

"No," said Mother, "not Father even. He went out early. No one else has been here."

"Only the snow giant," said Mary-Mary.

"Oh, don't be silly," said Martyn, and went out again.

Mary-Mary could hear the others all whispering together outside the back door. "It must have been a burglar!" "Let's find out where he went!" "Don't let Mary-Mary come – she'll spoil it." "We'll track him down."

Then they all went creeping along to the garden again.

Mary-Mary stood on a chair and looked out of the kitchen window. She saw Miriam, Martyn, Mervyn, and Meg all walking in a line round the garden, putting their feet carefully into the big footprints she had left, one after the other, and she began laughing to herself because they looked as if they were playing Follow my Leader.

"Why don't you go out and play too?" said Mother.

So Mary-Mary went and put on her own coat and Wellingtons.

As she was going out the others all came along to the house again to find Mother. They stood in a row in the doorway, looking very solemn and mysterious.

Then Miriam said, "Mother, we think we ought to tell you – there's been a strange man walking in our garden, and we think he may have been a burglar."

"Good gracious!" said Mother. "How do you know?"

"It wasn't a burglar," said Mary-Mary. "It was the–"

"Be quiet, Mary-Mary," said the others.

"We tracked his footprints in the snow," said Martyn.

"Dearie me!" said Mother. "I wonder who it was."

"It was the snow giant," said Mary-Mary. "Once upon a time there was a huge, great snow giant and he–"

"Oh, be quiet, Mary-Mary," said all the others.

"He had huge great boots on," said Miriam.

("That's what I was going to say," said Mary-Mary.)

"He went into the shed," said Martyn.

("Yes so did the snow giant," said Mary-Mary.)

"And came out again," said Mervyn.

("So did the snow giant," said Mary-Mary.)

"And walked all the way round the garden," said Meg.

("So did the–")

"BE QUIET, Mary-Mary," they all shouted.

"No," said Mother, "don't shout like that. If Mary-Mary wants to tell us something let her. What is it, Mary-Mary?"

"Well," said Mary-Mary, "once upon a time there was a huge, great snow giant –"

"There's no such thing," said Miriam.

"– and he came in the garden early in the morning–"

"Not *our garden*," said Martyn.

"– and he sat down in the middle of the lawn–"

"I don't believe it," said Mervyn.

"– and had snow for breakfast and–"

"Rubbish," said Meg.

"No, don't interrupt," said Mother. "Go on, Mary-Mary."

But Mary-Mary was getting cross at being interrupted so much; so she finished off by saying very quickly and loudly, "– and then four silly great children who thought they knew everything came walking into the garden, and they were all rather cross and grumbly, and all their names began with an M. They were called Mumbling, Muttering, Moaning, and – and Mumps, and when the snow giant saw them all grumbling round the garden he–"

But the others all shouted, "Be *quiet*, Mary-Mary! Why don't you go and play in the front garden and leave us alone?"

So Mary-Mary said, "All right, I will. I thought you wanted to know, but if you don't want to know I won't tell you." And she walked away with her nose in the air.

The snow in the front was nice and thick, and no one had trodden on it except down the path. Mary-Mary decided to make a real snow giant, just outside the sitting-room window.

"Then they'll *have* to believe in him," she said, "when they see him looking in at the window."

She began making a big pile of snow under the window, and was still hard at work when the postman came in at the gate.

"Hallo," he said. "What are you making?"

Mary-Mary told him. "Would you like to help?" she asked.

The postman said, no, he was sorry he couldn't help because he'd got work to do. But, all the same, he stopped long enough to show her how to roll some really big snowballs and pile them, one on top of the other, under the window; and soon the snow giant was as high as the window-sill.

"I must be off now," said the postman; "but that's quite a nice start for a snowman."

"Thank you very much," said Mary-Mary. "You *have* helped me a lot. If I wasn't so busy I'd help you take the letters round."

"That's all right," said the postman. "Any day will do for that. You don't get snow every day." And he went off, laughing.

The next person to come in at the gate was the milk-boy. He whistled when he saw the big pile of snow and said, "What's that going to be — a snowman?"

"A snow giant," said Mary-Mary.

"It wants to be bigger than that, then," said the milk-boy.

"Yes, it does," said Mary-Mary. "Would you like to help make it bigger?"

"What, me?" said the milk-boy. "Oh, no, I've got work to do."

But, all the same, he rolled up his sleeves and set to work to show Mary-Mary how to do it, and in a few minutes the snow giant reached half-way up the window. The milk-boy stepped back, puffing and blowing and wiping his face on a big red handkerchief.

"That's going to be a bit of all right," he said. "But I must be off."

"Thank you very much," said Mary-Mary. "You *have* helped me a lot. If I wasn't so busy I'd help you with the milk-bottles."

"That's all right," said the milk-boy. "Any old day will do for that." And he ran off up the road after the milk-cart.

Mary-Mary looked at the snow giant and decided he was tall enough now. All he needed was his head. She wasn't big enough to reach up, not even if she stood on the window-sill; so she decided to make it separately and ask some one else to lift it up when it was finished.

She rolled a very big snowball to the middle of the front gate and patted it smooth. Then she put two pebbles in for eyes, a lump of snow for a nose, and a twig from the hedge to make a mouth. It began to look very jolly. Mary-Mary laughed and put her own woolly cap on top. Then she picked some small green branches from the hedge and stuck them into the snowball all round the edges of the woolly cap. They looked just like hair. Then she made some eyebrows as well, to match.

A van drew up in front of the house, and a delivery man got down and came to the front gate with a big box under his arm. He grinned at Mary-Mary sitting in the snow by the great big snowball. Then he rested the box on the wall for a moment, and began writing in a little notebook.

"I'm sorry my snow giant's head is in the way," said Mary-Mary.

"That's all right," said the man. "I expect I can step over it."

"He's got a body over there," said Mary-Mary, pointing to it.

"That's nice," said the man, still writing.

"I think he'd really rather his head was on his body," said Mary-Mary. "It would be much easier for him than having it kicking around by the gate, wouldn't it?"

"Yes, I expect it would," said the delivery man.

"It's so much nicer to be all in one piece, don't you think?" said Mary-Mary.

"Yes, much nicer," said the man.

"So he'd be awfully glad if you'd do it for him," said Mary-Mary.

The man shut his little book, put his pencil behind his ear, and picked up the box again.

"*If* you would be so kind," said Mary-Mary very politely, and, getting up quickly, she stood in front of the snowball so that the man couldn't step over it.

"Eh?" said the man. "What do you want me to do?"

"Put his head on for him, please," said Mary-Mary. "He can't do it himself and I'm not tall enough to reach."

"Oh, I see!" said the man, laughing. "Yes, I'll do it for you. Which way round do you want him?"

"Looking in, please," said Mary-Mary. "I want him to give my big brothers and sisters a very small fright, because they said they didn't believe in him."

The delivery man looked at the side of the snowball which had the face on it.

"Oh, yes, he's a fine fellow," he said. "I don't think he'll frighten them much. He's got a nice smile."

"Yes, hasn't he?" said Mary-Mary. "I made it. It's a

twig really.''

The delivery man lifted the snow giant's head very carefully and put it on top of the snow giant's body in front of the sitting-room window. One of the pebble eyes fell out, and some of the green hair came out from under the woolly cap; but he lifted Mary-Mary up, and she put them back in the right places.

Then Mary-Mary said, ''Thank you very much. You *have* helped me a lot. Shall I help you do your deliveries?''

But the man said, no, there was no need, because he only had to drive the van from house to house delivering packages.

When the delivery man had driven away again, Mother made a hot chocolate drink and called all the children in from the garden.

Miriam, Martyn, Mervyn, and Meg came in, stamping the snow from their boots and blowing on their cold fingers.

"Well, how did you all get on?" said Mother.

"We haven't finished yet," said Miriam. "We spent such a lot of time looking for the burglar."

"There wasn't any burglar," said Mary-Mary.

"How do *you* know?" said the others.

"Because I know who it was," said Mary-Mary.

"Look here – *do* you know anything about it?" said Martyn.

"Of course I do," said Mary-Mary.

"Who was it, then?"

"I told you," said Mary-Mary. "It was the snow gi–"

"Oh, yes, I know all about your old snow giant," said Martyn. "But who was it really?"

"Me, of course," said Mary-Mary.

"But they were huge, great footprints!" said Miriam.

"I know," said Mary-Mary. "I had Father's boots on.

That's why I was being a snow giant, and I *did* sit down in the middle of the lawn and I *did* eat some snow.''

''*Well*, you might have told us!'' said Martyn.

''Well, really,'' said Mother. ''I do think you're all rather silly. Mary-Mary tried to tell you over and over again, but you just wouldn't listen.''

''Yes, but she kept on talking about a snow giant,'' they said; ''and we knew there was no such thing.''

''But there *is*,'' said Mary-Mary, ''and if you don't believe me go into the sitting-room and have a look.''

''Into the *sitting*-room!'' said Mother. 'Oh, Mary-Mary, what *have* you been doing? Surely you haven't brought a whole lot of snow into the house! Oh, dear! Oh, dear!''

And she ran along the passage, with the others all following, and opened the door into the sitting-room. Then Mary-Mary heard Mother laughing and laughing, and she heard the others all saying, ''Oh, my goodness!'' ''How did she do it?'' ''Isn't it huge?'' and

"I bet some one helped her!"

Then Mary-Mary began laughing too, and ran after them all. And when she saw her snow giant smiling in at the window with his twiggy mouth and his pebble eyes and his green-leaf hair sticking out from under the woolly cap she laughed more than ever, because he really did look so splendid and surprising.

"Well," said Mother, "I think you'll all have to agree that Mary-Mary's snow giant is quite the best thing in the garden!"

And they all had to agree that he was, and Mary-Mary was so pleased with herself that she turned head over heels nine times running, all round the sitting-room floor.

"The trouble with Mary-Mary is she's much too big for her boots," said Martyn.

"Oh, no!" said Mary-Mary, surprised. "The boots were much too big for me."

So there was a snow giant in Mary-Mary's garden, after all, and that is the end of the story.

DANNY FOX STEALS SOME FISH

David Thomson

Danny Fox lived in a small cave on the side of a mountain near the sea. He had a wife called Doxie and three children who were always hungry. Danny and Doxie were often hungry too. The names of their children were Lick, Chew, and Swallow.

Out on the mountain it was very cold, but in the cave it was warm and snug and Danny Fox liked to sleep curled up, with his nose tucked under his hind leg and his long bushy tail round his face like a scarf. Mrs Doxie Fox liked to sleep curled up, with her nose tucked underneath Lick's chin and her front legs hugging Chew and her hind legs hugging Swallow. And Lick, Chew, and Swallow liked to sleep curled up like furry balls against their mother's tummy, while she covered their backs with her long bushy tail like a scarf.

One day the little foxes woke up early and began to whine and yelp and howl.

"Why are you whining, Lick?" said Mrs Doxie Fox.

"I'm whining because I have nothing to lick," said Lick to his mother, Mrs Doxie Fox.

"Why are you yelping, Chew?" said Mrs Doxie Fox.

"I'm yelping because I have nothing to chew," said

Chew to his mother.

"Why are you howling, Swallow?" said Mrs Doxie Fox.

"I'm howling because I have nothing to swallow," said Swallow.

"Oh, please stop whining and yelping and howling," said Mrs Doxie Fox, "and I'll ask your father to fetch some food. Wake up, Danny Fox. It is time to go hunting."

"I'm not awake yet," said Danny Fox, and his voice sounded muffled underneath his bushy tail.

"Then how did you hear what I said?" said Mrs Doxie Fox.

"I heard you in my sleep," said Danny Fox. "And now I'm talking in my sleep." But he opened one eye and they knew he was only pretending. Lick, Chew, and Swallow thought he wasn't going to move, so they began their hullabaloo again.

"Oh, please fetch some food," said Mrs Doxie Fox. "Lick, Chew, and Swallow need something to lick, chew and swallow, and I need something too."

Danny Fox sat up and yawned. He stretched out his front legs and yawned and he stretched out his hind legs and yawned. Then he put his nose outside the cave and sniffed the cold air.

"Sniff, sniff. I can sniff a rabbit." He began to run faster and faster up the mountainside, sniffing the ground. Then he saw the rabbit, and yelped and ran faster than ever. But the rabbit escaped by diving into a crack between two rocks. The crack was too narrow for

Danny.

He trotted along and he trotted along. Then suddenly he stood quite still, with his bushy tail stretched out behind him and his long, smooth nose stretched out in front.

"Sniff, sniff. I can sniff a pigeon." He looked and he looked and he saw a wood-pigeon just below him on the hill, pecking at the ground. He walked very quietly, one step at a time. Then suddenly he sprang at the pigeon. But the pigeon saw him just in time and flew away, and Danny turned head over heels and rolled down the hill.

"Sniff, sniff," said Danny at the bottom of the hill. "I can sniff a mouse." But the mouse ran into its hole.

He trotted along and he trotted along till he came to a farm at the foot of the mountain.

"Sniff, sniff. I can sniff a hen." But the hen saw him and flew up to a branch of a tree.

"Sniff, sniff. I can sniff a duck." But the duck waddled into the farmer's house, where Danny was afraid to go.

"Sniff, sniff. I can sniff a goose." But the goose made such a noise that the farmer came out to see what was wrong and Danny had to hide beneath a bush. "I am unlucky this morning," he said to himself. "What can I find to take home?"

When the farmer had gone, he sneaked out of the farmyard and began to trot along the road. The road went along by the sea-shore, from the harbour to the town.

"Sniff, sniff. That's funny. I can sniff a fish."

Danny trotted along and he trotted along, feeling very hungry. The smell of fish got stronger and stronger, and the more he smelt it the hungrier he grew. His mouth watered, his pink tongue hung out and saliva dribbled from it on the road. He sniffed and sniffed and began to run fast. Then he came round a corner and suddenly stopped.

He saw a horse and cart in front of him. The horse was walking very slowly, the driver seemed to be asleep and the cart was loaded with boxes of fish, all gleaming silver.

Danny Fox walked very quietly, one step at a time. Then he ran very quietly with his bushy tail stretched

46

out behind him and his long smooth nose pointing up towards the cart. When he was near enough he sprang on to the cart and grabbed a fish from one of the open boxes. The driver did not look round. Danny Fox lay down very quietly, hoping not to wake him. His plan was to eat one fish, then pick up as many as he could hold in his mouth and jump off the cart and run home with them. He took a little mouthful of fish and the driver did not look round. He took a bigger mouthful of fish and the driver did not look round. Danny Fox watched him for a moment and saw that his hair was black and curly. He looked young and slim and strong.

"What a pity," thought Danny. "I wish he was old and slow!" And he lay down very quietly, hoping not to wake him. And crunch, crunch, crunch, he took a

great big noisy mouthful and the driver jumped up and brought his whip down – swish! – on the white tip of his tail. Danny Fox leapt off the cart and over a stone wall into a field.

Now he was very unhappy. He had eaten three mouthfuls of fish, but had nothing to bring home to Lick, Chew, and Swallow, and nothing for Doxie either. The cart had gone on but – "sniff, sniff, sniff" – he could still smell the fish as he lay hiding behind the wall.

He lay and he lay and he thought and he thought, till he thought of a plan. Then he got up quickly and he ran and he ran, keeping close behind the wall so that the driver of the cart could not see him. He ran till he came to a place where the road turned a corner, and by now the cart was far behind him. Then he jumped over the wall and lay down in the middle of the road pretending to be dead.

He lay there a long time. He heard the cart coming nearer and nearer. He kept his eyes shut. He hoped the driver would see him and not run him over.

When the driver saw Danny lying stretched in the middle of the road, he stopped his cart and said, "That's funny. That's the fox that was stealing my fish. That's the fox I hit with my whip. I thought I had only touched the tip of his tail, but now I see I must have hurt him badly. He must have run away from me ahead of my cart. And now he is dead." He got down from his cart and stooped to look at Danny.

"What a beautiful red coat he's got," the driver said,

"and what beautiful, thick red trousers. What a beautiful long bushy tail, with a beautiful white tip. What a beautiful long smooth nose with a beautiful black tip. I'll take him home with me, I think, and skin him and sell his fur."

So he picked up Danny Fox and threw him on to the cart on top of the boxes of fish. The cart went on. Danny opened one eye and saw the driver's back was turned to him. Then very quietly, he slid the tip of his tail underneath a fish and flicked it on to the road. He lay quite still and threw another fish out with his tail,

then another and another and another, till all down the road behind the cart there was a long, long line of fish stretching into the distance. And the driver never looked round because he thought Danny was dead. At the next corner, Danny jumped off the cart and ran back down the road. When the cart was out of sight, he started to pick the fish up.

He picked up one for Lick. He picked up one for Chew. He picked up one for Swallow. He tried to pick up one for Doxie too but his mouth was too full, so off he ran towards home with three fishes' heads sticking

out from one side of his mouth and three fishes' tails sticking out from the other.

He ran past the farm, and the duck and the goose and the hen were watching him.

"Look out," said the duck. "There goes Danny Fox!"

"That's funny," said the goose, "he has grown new whiskers."

"Those aren't whiskers," said the hen.

"Yes, they are," said the goose.

"No, they're not," said the hen.

"What are they, then?" said the duck.

"They are three fishes' heads on one side of his mouth," said the hen, "and three fishes' tails on the other."

Danny ran along the bottom of the mountain past the mouse's hole. The mouse was peeping out.

"That's funny," said the mouse. "I can see three fishes running along. But they have legs like a fox."

"Fishes don't have legs," said the pigeon who was flying up above.

"Yes, they do," said the mouse.

"No, they don't," said the pigeon.

"These ones do," said the mouse.

Danny Fox ran up the mountain past the crack in the rocks where the rabbit was hiding.

"That's funny," said the rabbit. "Danny Fox has been out fishing. I didn't know he had a boat."

At last Danny reached home. He threw one fish to Lick, and one fish to Chew and one fish to Swallow and while they were licking and chewing and swallowing he said to their mother, "Come quickly with me."

Doxie and Danny Fox ran down the mountain again till they came to the road — and after they had eaten three fish each, they picked up three fish each and carried them home. Then they went back for another three fish each, and another three fish each and another three fish each. They went on all morning carrying fish up the mountain, until there were no more left on the road.

So Danny and Doxie and Lick and Chew and Swallow had an enormous feast. They ate and they ate until they could eat no more. Then they all fell down together in a heap, fast asleep.

OLD ROGER IS DEAD

Traditional

Old Roger is dead and is laid in his grave,
      Laid in his grave,
      Laid in his grave;
Old Roger is dead and is laid in his grave,
      He, hi! laid in his grave.

There grew an old apple tree over his head,
      Over his head,
      Over his head;
There grew an old apple tree over his head,
      He, hi! over his head.

The apples grew ripe, and they all fell off,
      They all fell off,
      They all fell off;
The apples grew ripe, and they all fell off,
      He, hi! they all fell off.

There came an old woman a-picking them up,
     Picking them up,
     Picking them up;
There came an old woman a-picking them up,
     He, hi! picking them up.

Old Roger jumps up and he gives her a knock,
     Gives her a knock,
     Gives her a knock;
Old Roger jumps up and he gives her a knock,
     He, hi! gives her a knock.

He makes the old woman go hipperty hop,
     Hipperty hop,
     Hipperty hop;
He makes the old woman go hipperty hop,
     He, hi! hipperty hop.

THE OLD WOMAN AND HER PIG

An English folktale

RETOLD BY JOSEPH JACOBS

An old woman was sweeping her house, and she found a little crooked sixpence. "What," said she, "shall I do with this little sixpence? I will go to market, and buy a little pig."

As she was coming home, she came to a stile: but the piggy wouldn't go over the stile.

She went a little further, and she met a dog. So she said to him: "Dog! dog! bite pig; piggy won't go over the stile and I shan't get home to-night." But the dog wouldn't.

She went a little further, and she met a stick. So she said: "Stick! stick! beat dog! dog won't bite pig; piggy won't get over the stile and I shan't get home to-night." But the stick wouldn't.

56

She went a little further, and she met a fire. So she said: "Fire! fire! burn stick; stick won't beat dog; dog won't bite pig; piggy won't get over the stile and I shan't get home to-night." But the fire wouldn't.

She went a little further, and she met some water. So she said: "Water! water! quench fire; fire won't burn stick; stick won't beat dog; dog won't bite pig; piggy won't get over the stile and I shan't get home to-night." But the water wouldn't.

She went a little further, and she met an ox. So she said: "Ox! ox! drink water; water won't quench fire; fire won't burn stick; stick won't beat dog; dog won't bite pig; piggy won't get over the stile and I shan't get home to-night." But the ox wouldn't.

She went a little further, and she met a butcher. So she said: "Butcher! butcher! kill ox; ox won't drink water; water won't quench fire; fire won't burn stick; stick won't beat dog; dog won't bite pig; piggy won't get over the stile and I shan't get home to-night." But the butcher wouldn't.

She went a little further, and she met a rope. So she said: "Rope! rope! hang butcher; butcher won't kill ox; ox won't drink water; water won't quench fire; fire won't burn stick; stick won't beat dog; dog won't bite pig; piggy won't get over the stile and I shan't get home to-night." But the rope wouldn't.

She went a little further, and she met a rat. So she said: "Rat! rat! gnaw rope: rope won't hang butcher; butcher won't kill ox; ox won't drink water; water won't quench fire; fire won't burn stick; stick won't

beat dog; dog won't bite pig; piggy won't get over the stile and I shan't get home to-night." But the rat wouldn't.

She went a little further, and she met a cat. So she said: "Cat! cat! kill rat; rat won't gnaw rope; rope won't hang butcher; butcher won't kill ox; ox won't drink water; water won't quench fire; fire won't burn stick; stick won't beat dog; dog won't bite pig; piggy won't get over the stile and I shan't get home to-night." But the cat said to her: "If you will go to yonder cow, and fetch me a saucer of milk, I will kill the rat." So away went the old woman to the cow.

But the cow said to her: "If you will go to yonder hay-stack, and fetch me a handful of hay, I'll give you the milk." So away went the old woman to the hay-stack; and she brought the hay to the cow.

As soon as the cow had eaten the hay, she gave the old woman the milk; and away she went with it in a saucer to the cat.

As soon as the cat had lapped up the milk, the cat began to kill the rat; the rat began to gnaw the rope; the rope began to hang the butcher; the butcher began to kill the ox; the ox began to drink the water; the water began to quench the fire; the fire began to burn the stick; the stick began to beat the dog; the dog began to bite the pig; the little pig in a fright jumped over the stile, and so the old woman got home that night.

THE LITTLE WOMAN'S WATER-POT

Lilian Daykin

Early one morning, a little African girl woke on her sleeping mat. She stretched and yawned when she heard her big sister, Deda, pounding maize into meal and singing. Zua wished she was big enough to pound maize. It sounded great fun.

But when Zua stood in the doorway of the round African house, she didn't look at her sister. No, she stared at Mboni, her mother, with unblinking round eyes, wondering whatever she could be making with so small a lump of clay.

"What do you make, Mama?" she asked curiously.

Mboni looked up.

"What do you think it is, my Brightness?"

Zua looked at the small lump of red clay in her mother's hands, wondering and wondering. Then she shook her curly head.

"It can't be a cooking-pot. It's far too small."

"It's *not* a cooking-pot," agreed Mboni, pressing her fist deep into the centre of the clay. Then she moulded the red clay into the shape of a jar with a narrow rim, turning and smoothing it with her strong, clay-stained

hands.

"And it can't be a water-pot. It's far too small for that either," said Zua.

Mboni laughed.

"But it *is* a water-pot, Zua. A little water-pot for a little woman."

"She must be a very little woman if she can only carry a water-pot that size." Zua sounded puzzled. "I've never seen a woman as small as that, never."

Deda laughed merrily.

"Ho! Ho! Just hark at Zua. She's never seen a little woman."

Zua hated to be laughed at.

"Well, have you, Deda?"

"Oh, many, many times," answered Deda, chuckling to herself as she gave the maize a final bang.

"Will you show me this little woman, Mama?" pleaded Zua, feeling very curious.

"If all goes well, you shall certainly know her, my daughter," promised Mboni gently, and with that Zua had to be content, for neither her mother nor sister would tell her any more about the little woman.

Soon Mboni set the tiny water-pot to dry in the sun. It looked very, very small beside the other water-pots and cooking-pots waiting to be baked.

"Don't touch the little water-pot, Zua. It is still very soft."

As Mboni spoke, they heard Granny calling from her house not very far away.

"Mboni, Mboni, are you ready? It is time to fetch wood for the firing tomorrow."

All the women of the village hurried off with hatchet, bush-knife and bark-string. Zua rode on her mother's back, for it was a long way to the forest.

"Why doesn't that little woman make her own water-pots, Mama?" whispered Zua in her mother's ear."

"She's far too small, Zua."

"Is the little woman smaller than Deda?"

"Yes, much smaller. She can't even pound her own maize," said Mboni. "Now, Zua, see how big you can make your bundle of wood for the pot-firing."

On the way home that afternoon, Zua had her own burden of wood to carry. She walked before her mother and sister proudly balancing it on her head without once touching it with her hands, just as they had taught her.

"Behold our little Brightness! Does she not bear her burden well?" said Mboni to Deda and their bright eyes gleamed with pride in their little one.

When all the wood had been placed round the firing-pit behind the village, Granny was satisfied. "It is good!" she said. "We have enough wood to fire many pots."

Next morning while Mboni polished her unbaked pots with a pebble, Deda and Zua went to collect leaves for the firing-pit. It was great fun carrying huge banana leaves to use for lining the pit.

In the late afternoon when the sun was not so hot, Mboni called her daughters.

"Deda, Zua, it is time for the great firing. Come, help me to prepare the pots."

The girls helped to pile the pots on top of each other, with leaves between each so that they should not be broken.

"I'll take the large cooking-pot," said Mboni. "Zua can carry the little woman's water-pot."

"What, me?" asked Zua in great astonishment.

Mboni smiled.

"Yes, you, Zua. If you can carry wood you can carry water-pots, but be careful or the little woman will lose her water-pot before it is fired."

Zua was careful, very careful. This was the first time she'd carried a water-pot on her head. It was much more difficult than carrying wood, for it might break if she let it drop.

"Look at Zua!" exclaimed Granny. "Isn't she a clever girl!"

Zua glowed with delight and showed every one of her white teeth in a large smile, as she proudly walked through the village bearing her small burden.

Mboni placed the little woman's water-pot with the larger ones on the mound of leaves in the firing-pit. Then she helped Granny and the Aunts to fill all the pots with leaves and twigs and cover them with more leaves and wood. Then the large logs were piled into a high tower over the hidden pots. The time of firing had come!

Granny brought embers from her own fire in a broken crock and laid them on the dry leaves in the pit. The women knelt down and blew hard at the embers. The leaves spluttered, crackled and smoked, then out burst many flames at once. A lovely sight!

''The Great Fire is lit!'' shouted the children, jumping up and down in their excitement.

But Zua sat quietly beside her mother, watching the flames. ''Please, fire, be kind to the little water-pot, make it hard, make it strong, to carry water for the little woman,'' she said softly.

Soon even the big logs were blazing and the heart of the fire glowed like a furnace. It was so hot that the women and children had to draw back or the heat would have burnt them.

Tired with all the excitement, Zua fell asleep. When

she awoke she saw her mother lifting a small pot out of the glowing mound of white wood-ash.

"The little woman's water-pot!" she shouted. "Oh, do be careful, Mama!"

"Don't touch, Zua, it must cool first," explained Mboni.

It seemed a long time to the little girl before her mother picked up the little water-pot and flicked it with her finger-nail.

"Ping! Ping!" sang the little water-pot.

"Hark, Zua!" said Mboni, flicking the little water-pot again. "Ping! Ping! It rings as true as a bell. It has fired perfectly. Not a crack, not a blister. It's the most beautiful water-pot I have ever made."

"Won't the little woman be pleased!" cried Zua.

So a trail of women padded homewards on their hard-soled feet, each carrying a pile of newly-fired pots. But none was prouder than Zua carrying the little woman's water-pot on her own head.

Zua's father stood waiting at the door of their home.

"Well! Well!" he exclaimed. "What a day for rejoicing! If it isn't the little woman, Zua, with her very first water-pot on her head. Welcome home, my own little woman!"

Then Zua's heart glowed with delight. At last she knew who the little woman was who was too small to make her own water-pot. It was herself!

AS I WAS GOING TO ST IVES

Traditional

As I was going to St Ives,
I met a man with seven wives,
Each wife had seven sacks,
Each sack had seven cats,
Each cat had seven kits,
Kits, cats, sacks and wives,
How many were going to St Ives?

THE ENORMOUS TURNIP

Aleksei Tolstoy

RETOLD BY SUSAN DICKINSON

Once there was an old man and an old woman. All around their little old house they grew vegetables: peas, beans and marrows to eat in the summer; and potatoes, carrots, onions and turnips to eat in the winter.

One day the old man went out to weed his rows of turnips, and he saw that one turnip was bigger than all the rest. The turnip grew bigger, and bigger, and bigger. Until the day came when the old man decided to pull it up. He pulled and he pulled, but the turnip stayed fast in the ground.

The old man called the old woman.

The old woman pulled the old man.

The old man pulled the turnip. They pulled and pulled but they could not pull it up.

The old woman called the grand-daughter.

The grand-daughter pulled the old woman.

The old woman pulled the old man.

The old man pulled the turnip. They pulled and pulled, but they could not pull it up.

The grand-daughter called the dog.

The dog pulled the grand-daughter.

The grand-daughter pulled the old woman.

The old woman pulled the old man.

The old man pulled the turnip. They pulled and pulled but they could not pull it up.

The dog called the cat.

The cat pulled the dog.

The dog pulled the grand-daughter.

The grand-daughter pulled the old woman.

The old woman pulled the old man.

The old man pulled the turnip. They pulled and pulled but they could not pull it up.

The cat called the mouse.

The mouse pulled the cat.

The cat pulled the dog.

The dog pulled the grand-daughter.

The grand-daughter pulled the old woman.

The old woman pulled the old man.

The old man pulled the turnip. They pulled and pulled, and pulled and pulled and pulled. And up came the turnip at last!

And the old woman and the grand-daughter cut the turnip into a thousand pieces.

HENNY-PENNY

An English folktale

RETOLD BY JOSEPH JACOBS

One day Henny-penny was picking up corn in the cornyard when – whack! – something hit her upon the head. "Goodness gracious me!" said Henny-penny; "the sky's a-going to fall; I must go and tell the king."

So she went along, and she went along, and she went along till she met Cocky-locky. "Where are you going, Henny-penny?" says Cocky-locky. "Oh! I'm going to tell the king the sky's a-falling," says Henny-penny. "May I come with you?" says Cocky-locky. "Certainly," says Henny-penny. So Henny-penny and Cocky-locky went to tell the king the sky was falling.

They went along, and they went along, and they went along till they met Ducky-daddles. "Where are you going to, Henny-penny and Cocky-locky?" says Ducky-daddles. "Oh! we're going to tell the king the sky's a-falling," said Henny-penny and Cocky-locky. "May I come with you?" says Ducky-daddles. "Certainly," said Henny-penny and Cocky-locky. So Henny-penny, Cocky-locky and Ducky-daddles went to tell the king the sky was a-falling.

So they went along, and they went along, and they went along till they met Goosey-poosey. "Where are you going to, Henny-penny, Cocky-locky and Ducky-daddles?'' said Goosey-poosey. "Oh! we're going to tell the king the sky's a-falling,'' said Henny-penny and Cocky-locky and Ducky-daddles. "May I come with you?'' said Goosey-poosey. "Certainly,'' said Henny-penny, Cocky-locky and Ducky-daddles. So Henny-penny, Cocky-locky, Ducky-daddles and Goosey-poosey went to tell the king the sky was falling.

So they went along, and they went along, and they went along till they met Turkey-lurkey. "Where are

you going, Henny-penny, Cocky-locky, Ducky-daddles and Goosey-poosey?" says Turkey-lurkey. "Oh!
we're going to tell the king the sky's a-falling," said
Henny-penny, Cocky-locky, Ducky-daddles and Goosey-poosey. "May I come with you, Henny-penny,
Cocky-locky, Ducky-daddles and Goosey-poosey?"
said Turkey-lurkey. "Oh, certainly, Turkey-lurkey,"
said Henny-penny, Cocky-locky, Ducky-daddles and
Goosey-poosey. So Henny-penny, Cocky-locky, Ducky-
daddles, Goosey-poosey and Turkey-lurkey went to
tell the king the sky was falling.

So they went along, and they went along, and they
went along till they met Foxy-woxy, and Foxy-woxy
said to Henny-penny, Cocky-locky, Ducky-daddles,
Goosey-poosey and Turkey-lurkey: "Where are you
going, Henny-penny, Cocky-locky, Ducky-daddles,
Goosey-poosey and Turkey-lurkey?" And Henny-
penny, Cocky-locky, Ducky-daddles, Goosey-poosey
and Turkey-lurkey said to Foxy-woxy: "We're going to
tell the king the sky's a-falling." "Oh! but this is not the

way to the king, Henny-penny, Cocky-locky, Ducky-daddles, Goosey-poosey and Turkey-lurkey," says Foxy-woxy; "I know the proper way. Shall I show it you?" "Oh certainly, Foxy-woxy," said Henny-penny, Cocky-locky, Ducky-daddles, Goosey-poosey and Turkey-lurkey. So Henny-penny, Cocky-locky, Ducky-daddles, Goosey-poosey, Turkey-lurkey, and Foxy-woxy all went to tell the king the sky was a-falling.

So they went along, and they went along, and they went along till they came to a narrow and dark hole. Now this was the door of Foxy-woxy's cave. But Foxy-woxy said to Henny-penny, Cocky-locky, Ducky-daddles, Goosey-poosey and Turkey-lurkey: "This is the short way to the king's palace: you'll soon get there if you follow me. I will go first and you come after, Henny-penny, Cocky-locky, Ducky-daddles, Goosey-poosey and Turkey-lurkey." "Why, of course, certainly, without doubt, why not?" said Henny-penny, Cocky-locky, Ducky-daddles, Goosey-poosey and Turkey-lurkey.

So Foxy-woxy went into his cave, and he didn't go very far but turned round to wait for Henny-penny, Cocky-locky, Ducky-daddles, Goosey-poosey and Turkey-lurkey. First Turkey-lurkey went through the dark hole into the cave. He hadn't got far when ''Hrumph'', Foxy-woxy snapped off Turkey-lurkey's head and threw his body over his left shoulder. Then Goosey-poosey went in, and ''Hrumph'', off went her head and Goosey-poosey was thrown beside Turkey-lurkey. Then Ducky-daddles waddled down, and ''Hrumph'', snapped Foxy-woxy, and Ducky-daddles' head was off and Ducky-daddles was thrown alongside Turkey-lurkey and Goosey-poosey. Then Cocky-locky strutted down into the cave and he hadn't gone far when ''Snap, Hrumph!'' went Foxy-woxy and Cocky-locky was thrown alongside Turkey-lurkey, Goosey-poosey and Ducky-daddles.

But Foxy-woxy had made two bites at Cocky-locky, and when the first snap only hurt Cocky-locky, but didn't kill him, he called out to Henny-penny. But she turned tail and off she ran home, so she never told the king the sky was a-falling.

HECTOR PROTECTOR

Traditional

Hector Protector was dressed all in green;
Hector Protector was sent to the Queen.
The Queen did not like him,
No more did the King,
So Hector Protector was sent back again.

BAGPIPES

Traditional

A cat came fiddling out of a barn,
With a pair of bagpipes under her arm;
She could sing nothing but fiddle cum fee,
The mouse has married the bumble bee.
Pipe cat! Dance mouse!
We'll have a wedding at our good house.

HOW THE HAT ASHES SHOVEL HELPED SNOO FOO

Carl Sandburg

If you want to remember the names of all six of the Sniggers children, remember that the three biggest were named Blink, Swink and Jink but the three littlest ones were named Blunk, Swunk and Junk. One day last January the three biggest had a fuss with the three littlest. The fuss was about a new hat for Snoo Foo, the snow man, about what kind of a hat he should wear and how he should wear it. Blink, Swink and Jink said, ''He wants a crooked hat put on straight.'' Blunk, Swunk and Junk said, ''He wants a straight hat put on crooked.'' They fussed and fussed. Blink fussed with Blunk, Swink fussed with Swunk, and Jink fussed with Junk. The first ones to make up after the fuss were Jink and Junk. They decided the best way to settle the fuss. ''Let's put a crooked hat on crooked,'' said Jink. ''No, let's put a straight hat on straight,'' said Junk. Then they stood looking and looking into each other's shiny laughing eyes and then both of them exploded to each other at the same time, ''Let's put on two hats, a crooked hat crooked and a straight hat straight.''

Well, they looked around for hats. But there were

not any hats anywhere, that is, no hats big enough for a snow man with a big head like Snoo Foo. So they went in the house and asked their mother for *the hat ashes shovel*. Of course, in most any other house, the mother would be all worried if six children came tramping and clomping in, banging the door and all six ejaculating to their mother at once, "Where is the hat ashes shovel?" But Missus Sniggers wasn't worried at all. She rubbed her chin with her finger and said softly, "Oh lah de dah, oh lah de dah, where is that hat ashes shovel, last week I had it when I was making a hat for Mister Sniggers; I remember I had that hat ashes shovel right up here over the clock, oh lah de dah, oh lah de dah. Go out and ring the front door bell," she said to Jink Sniggers. Jink ran away to the front door. And Missus Sniggers and the five children waited. Bling-bling the bell began ringing and – listen – the door of the clock opened and the hat ashes shovel fell out. "Oh lah de dah, get out of here in a hurry," said Missus Sniggers.

Well, the children ran out and dug a big pail of hat ashes with the hat ashes shovel. And they made two hats for Snoo Foo. One was a crooked hat. The other was a straight hat. And they put the crooked hat on crooked and the straight hat on straight. And there stood Snoo Foo in the front yard and everybody who came by on the street, he would take off his hat to them, the crooked hat with his arm crooked and the straight hat with his arm straight. That was the end of the fuss between the Sniggers children and it was Jink, the littlest one of the biggest, and Junk, the littlest one of the littlest, who settled the fuss by looking clean into each other's eyes and laughing. If you ever get into a fuss try this way of settling it.

MY NAUGHTY LITTLE SISTER AND FATHER CHRISTMAS

Dorothy Edwards

This is such a very terrible story about my naughty little sister that I hardly know how to tell it to you. It is all about one Christmas-time when I was a little girl, and my naughty little sister was a very little girl.

Now, my naughty little sister was very pleased when Christmas began to draw near, because she liked all the excitement of the plum-puddings and the turkeys, and the crackers and the holly, and all the Christmassy-looking shops, but there was one very awful thing about her – she didn't like to think about Father Christmas at all – she said he was a *horrid old man*!

There – I knew you would be shocked at that. But she did. And she said she wouldn't put up her stocking for him.

My mother told my naughty little sister what a good old man Father Christmas was, and how he brought the toys along on Christmas Eve, but my naughty little sister said, "I don't care. And I don't want that nasty old man coming to our house."

Well now, that was bad enough, wasn't it? But the really dreadful thing happened later on.

This is the dreadful thing: one day, my school-teacher said that a Father Christmas Man would be coming to the school to bring presents for all the children, and my teacher said that the Father Christmas Man would have toys for all our little brothers and sisters as well, if they cared to come along for them. She said that there would be a real Christmas-tree with candles on it, and sweeties and cups of tea and biscuits for our mothers.

Wasn't that a nice thought? Well now, when I told my little sister about the Christmas-tree, she said, "Oh, nice!"

And when I told her about the sweeties she said, "Very, very nice!" But when I told her about the Father Christmas Man, she said, "Don't want *him*, nasty old man."

Still, my mother said, "You can't go to the Christmas-tree without seeing him, so if you don't want to see him all that much, you will have to stay at home."

But my naughty little sister did want to go, very much, so she said, "I will go, and when the horrid Father Christmas Man comes in, I will close my eyes."

So, we all went to the Christmas-tree together, my mother and I, and my naughty little sister.

When we got to the school, my naughty little sister was very pleased to see all the pretty paper-chains that we had made in school hanging all round the class-rooms, and when she saw all the little lanterns, and the holly and all the robin-redbreast drawings pinned on the blackboards she smiled and smiled. She was very smily at first.

All the mothers, and the little brothers and sisters who were too young for school sat down in chairs and desks, and the big school-children acted a play for them.

My little sister was very excited to see all the children dressed up as fairies and robins and elves and bo-peeps and things, and she clapped her hands very hard, like all the grown-ups did, to show that she was enjoying herself. And she still smiled.

Then, when some of the teachers came round with bags of sweets, tied up in pretty coloured paper, my little sister smiled even more, and she sang too when all the children sang. She sang, "Away in a manger", because she knew the words very well. When she didn't know the words of some of the singing, she "la-la'd".

After all the singing, the teachers put out the lights, and took away a big screen from a corner of the room, and there was the Christmas-tree, all lit up with candles and shining with silvery stuff, and little shiny coloured balls. There were lots of toys on the tree, and

all the children cheered and clapped.

Then the teachers put the light on again, and blew out the candles, so that we could all go and look at the tree. My little sister went too. She looked at the tree, and she looked at the toys, and she saw a specially nice doll with a blue dress on, and she said, "For me."

My mother said, "You must wait and see what you are given."

Then the teachers called out, "Back to your seats, everyone, we have a visitor coming." So all the children went back to their seats, and sat still and waited and listened.

And, as we waited and listened, we heard a tinkle-tinkle bell noise, and then the schoolroom door opened, and in walked the Father Christmas Man. My naughty little sister had forgotten all about him, so she hadn't time to close her eyes before he walked in. However, when she saw him, my little sister stopped smiling and began to be stubborn.

The Father Christmas Man was very nice. He said he hoped we were having a good time, and we all said, "Yes," except my naughty little sister – she didn't say a thing.

Then he said, "Now, come up one at a time, children; and I will give each one of you a toy."

So, first of all each school-child went up for a toy, and my naughty little sister still didn't shut her eyes because she wanted to see who was going to have the specially nice doll in the blue dress. But none of the school-children had it.

Then Father Christmas began to call the little brothers and sisters up for presents, and, as he didn't know their names, he just said, "Come along, sonny," if it were a boy, and "come along, girlie," if it were a girl. The Father Christmas Man let the little brothers and sisters choose their own toys off the tree.

When my naughty little sister saw this, she was so worried about the specially nice doll, that she thought that she would just go up and get it. She said, "I don't like that horrid old beardy man, but I do like that nice doll."

So, my naughty little sister got up without being asked to, and she went right out to the front where the Father Christmas Man was standing, and she said, "That doll, please," and pointed to the doll she wanted.

The Father Christmas Man laughed and all the teachers laughed, and the other mothers and the school-children, and all the little brothers and sisters. My mother did not laugh because she was so shocked to see my naughty little sister going out without being asked to.

The Father Christmas Man took the specially nice doll off the tree, and he handed it to my naughty little sister and he said, "Well now, I hear you don't like me very much, but won't you just shake hands?" and my naughty little sister said, "No." But she took the doll all the same.

The Father Christmas Man put out his nice old hand for her to shake and be friends, and do you know what that naughty bad girl did? *She bit his hand*. She really and truly did. Can you think of anything more dreadful and terrible? She bit Father Christmas's good old hand, and then she turned and ran and ran out of the school with all the children staring after her, and her doll held very tight in her arms.

The Father Christmas Man was very nice, he said it wasn't a hard bite, only a frightened one, and he made all the children sing songs together.

When my naughty little sister was brought back by my mother, she said she was very·sorry, and the Father Christmas Man said, "That's all right, old lady," and because he was so smily and nice to her, my funny little sister went right up to him, and gave him a big "sorry" kiss, which pleased him very much.

And she hung her stocking up after all, and that kind man remembered to fill it for her.

My little sister kept the specially nice doll until she was quite grown-up. She called it Rosy-primrose, and although she was sometimes bad-tempered with it, she really loved it very much indeed.

ROLL OVER

Traditional

There were ten in the bed
And the little one said:
   "Roll over! Roll over!"
So they all rolled over,
And one fell out.

There were nine in the bed
And the little one said:
   "Roll over! Roll over!"
So they all rolled over,
And one fell out.

There were eight in the bed
And the little one said:
   "Roll over! Roll over!"
So they all rolled over,
And one fell out.

There were seven in the bed
And the little one said:
    "Roll over! Roll over!"
So they all rolled over,
And one fell out.

There were six in the bed
And the little one said:
    "Roll over! Roll over!"
So they all rolled over,
And one fell out.

There were five in the bed
And the little one said:
    "Roll over! Roll over!"
So they all rolled over,
And one fell out.

There were four in the bed
And the little one said:
    "Roll over! Roll over!"
So they all rolled over,
And one fell out.

There were three in the bed
And the little one said:
    "Roll over! Roll over!"
So they all rolled over,
And one fell out.

There were two in the bed
And the little one said:
    "Roll over! Roll over!"
So they all rolled over,
And one fell out.

There was one in the bed
And the little one said:
    "Roll over! Roll over!"
So HE rolled over,
And HE fell out.

So there was the bed –
And no one said
    "Roll over! Roll over!"

THE BUTTERFLY WHO SANG

Terry Jones

A butterfly was once sitting on a leaf looking extremely sad.

"What's wrong?" asked a friendly frog.

"Oh," said the butterfly, "nobody really appreciates me," and she parted her beautiful red and blue wings and shut them again.

"What d'you mean?" asked the frog. "I've seen you flying about and thought to myself: that is one hell of a beautiful butterfly! All my friends think you look great, too! You're a real stunner!"

"Oh, *that*," replied the butterfly, and she opened her wings again. "Who cares about my *looks*? It's my singing that nobody appreciates."

"I've never heard your singing: but if it's anywhere near as good as your looks, you've got it made!" said the frog.

"That's the trouble," replied the butterfly. "People say they can't hear my singing. I suppose it's so refined and so high that their ears aren't sensitive enough to pick it up."

"But I bet it's great all the same!" said the frog.

"It is," said the butterfly. "Would you like me to sing

for you?''

"Well . . . I don't suppose my ears are sensitive enough to pick it up, but I'll give it a try!'' said the frog.

So the butterfly spread her wings and opened her mouth. The frog gazed in wonder at the butterfly's beautiful wings, for he'd never been so close to them before.

The butterfly sang on and on, and still the frog gazed at her wings absolutely captivated, even though he could hear nothing whatsoever of her singing.

Eventually, however, the butterfly stopped, and closed up her wings.

"Beautiful!" said the frog, thinking about the wings.

"Thank you," said the butterfly, thrilled that at last she had found an appreciative listener.

After that, the frog came every day to listen to the butterfly sing, though all that time he was really feasting his eyes on her beautiful wings. And every day, the butterfly tried harder and harder to impress the frog with her singing, even though he could not hear a single note of it.

But one day a moth, who was jealous of all the attention the butterfly was getting, took the butterfly on one side and said: "Butterfly, your singing is quite superb."

"Thank you," said the butterfly.

"With just a little more practice," said the cunning moth, "you could be as famous a singer as the nightingale."

"Do you think so?" asked the butterfly, flattered beyond words.

"I certainly do," replied the moth. "Indeed, perhaps you already *do* sing better than the nightingale, only it's difficult to concentrate on your music because your gaudy wings are so distracting."

"Is that right?" said the butterfly.

"I'm afraid so," said the moth. "You notice the

nightingale is wiser, and wears only dull brown feathers so as not to distract from her singing."

"You're right!" cried the butterfly. "I was a fool not to have realized that before!"

And straight away she found some earth and rubbed it into her wings until they were all grey and half the colours had rubbed off.

The next day, the frog arrived for the concert as usual, but when the butterfly opened her wings he cried out: "Oh! Butterfly! What have you done to your beautiful wings?" And the butterfly explained what she had done.

"I think you will find," she said, "that now you will be able to concentrate more on my music."

Well, the poor frog tried, but it was no good, for of course he couldn't hear anything at all. So he soon became bored, and hopped off into the pond. And after that the butterfly never *could* find anyone to listen to her singing.

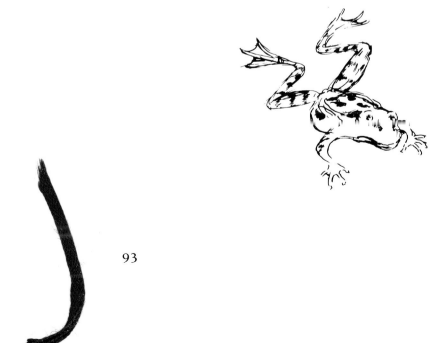